Roxy   Buddy   Max   Spot   SpikE

For Ezzy & Levon
—J.H.

ISBN 978-0-06-218970-7 (trade bdg.)

Design by Martha Rago. Hand lettering by James Horvath.

14 15 16 17 18 SCP 10 9 8 7 6 5 4 3 2 1

❖

First Edition

James Horvath

Work, Dogs, Work

A Highway Tail

HARPER

An Imprint of HarperCollinsPublishers

ill up your cups;
today's a big day.
We've got miles and miles
of new road to lay.

Load up the trucks.
It's time to get moving.
There's a road out there
that needs some improving.

This road's in bad shape
and in need of repair.
We'll fix it right up
from here to there.

We'll need a bulldozer

and a grader or two,

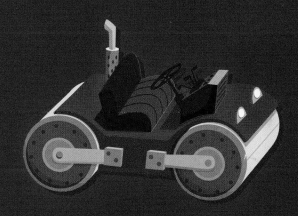

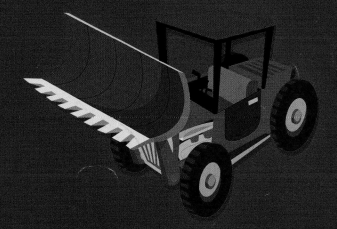

a steamroller,

a loader,

and a paving truck, too.

Bulldoze a path
and smooth it with graders—
no more bumps
from potholes and craters!

The steamrollers roll
heavy and slow.
They flatten and level
the dirt as they go.

Dump trucks rumble as
Duke makes the call:

"Head out to the quarry and

...haul, dogs, haul!"

The rock quarry is where
we get all of our stone.
The dump truck fills up
in the rock-loading zone.

Huge quarry trucks
are too big for the street.
To move tons of rock,
these trucks can't be beat.

The dump trucks dump
straight into the hopper.
The paver spreads asphalt
to a road height that's proper.

Dump trucks deliver
load after load.
It will take lots of trips
to build this long road.

The road crew is busy
arranging orange cones.
They help keep us safe
in construction zones.

Stop, dogs, stop!

You have to wait here.

Go, dogs, go!

The road is now clear.

We can't go through here;
our trucks will get stuck.
It's mile after mile of
axle-deep muck!

With hills on both sides,
Duke knows what to do.
"Get digging, dogs!
We must tunnel through!"

This rock is too hard
to dig our way through.
Time to bring in
the demolition crew!

Set the charges and
get out of there fast.

Shout, "Fire in the hole!" then

blast, dogs, blast!

Take cover now, stand clear,
make some room.
The tunnel blasts open
with a massive

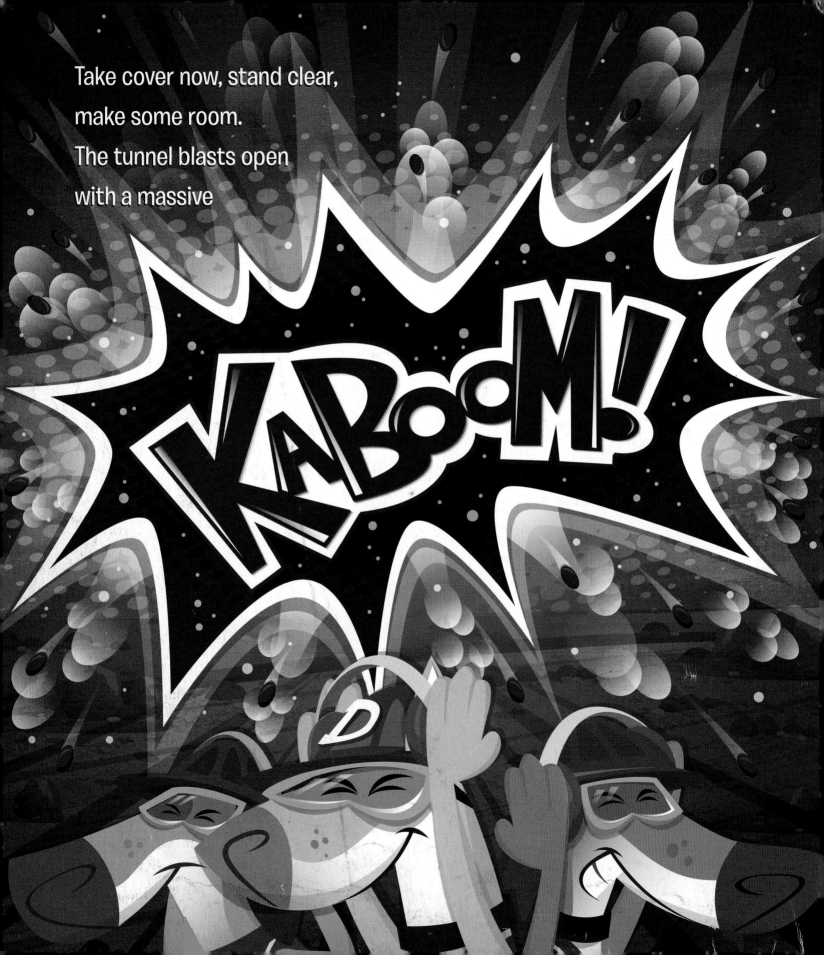

Clean up this rubble.

Let's haul it away.

Work, dogs, work!

There's more road to lay.